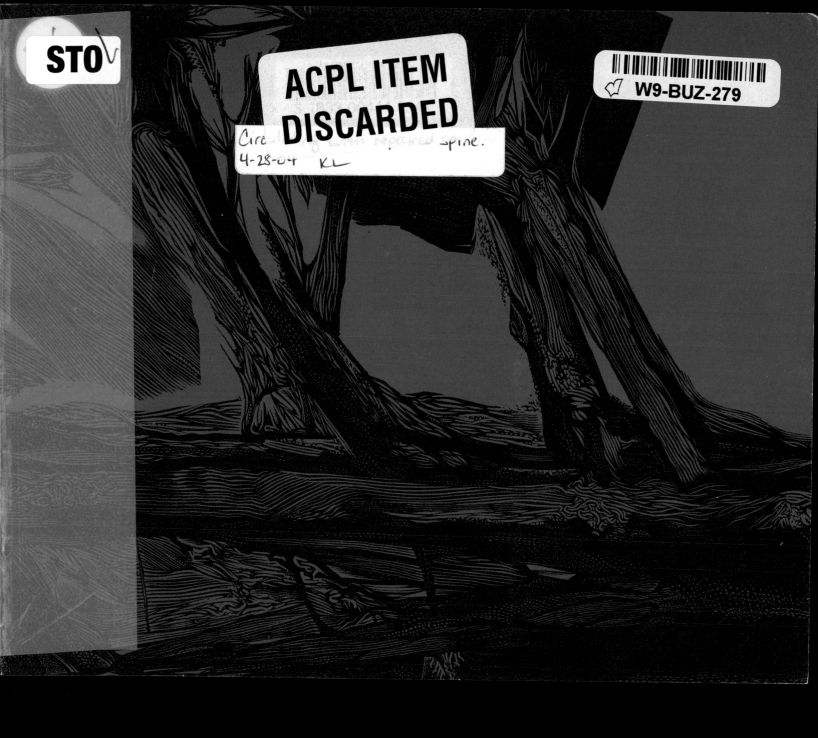

They Walk in the Night

BY ELIZABETH COATSWORTH

Lighthouse Island
Cricket and the Emperor's Son
Troll Weather
The Place
The Cat Who Went to Heaven
Ronnie and the Chief's Son
Alice All-by-Herself
The Captain's Daughter
The Cat and the Captain
The Little Haymakers
Sword of the Wilderness

Away Goes Sally
The Fair American
Five Bushel Farm
The Wishing Pear
Boston Bells
Old Whirlwind
The Sod House
They Walk in the Night
The Sparrow Bush
Poems
Summer Green

Elizabeth Coatsworth

They Walk in the Night

Wood engravings by Stefan Martin

W · W · NORTON & COMPANY · INC ·

New York

To all the household
at Chimney Farm

Author's Note

Alida's Africa will be found on no map. It is an Africa of the mind, but it is made up of elements of the real Africa where there are coffee plantations and rivers, sometimes flowing under forest trees, sometimes falling in rapids, sometimes widening as they come to the plains. Here graze the wild beasts that Alida saw, but the tame herd would be more likely to have been a herd of great-horned cattle rather than of horses. The magicians, I think, would not have worn their animal garments so openly. There are, or were, such secret societies, of which the leopard men were the most feared, tearing their victims to death with their steel claws. Would the antelope man have taken the risk of making such an enemy to rescue a stranger? In all parts of the earth there are men who take such risks, just as everyone, like Alida, must at some time set off on his or her voyage into the world. As for the mountain with the snowy crest like a star, did it really rise above Alida's house? Yes, for I put it there. Its beautiful name is Kilimanjaro.

Elizabeth Coatsworth
January, 1969

The leopard, the antelope,
  and the owl
Can see in the dark in the
  darkest night,
And the great snake staring from
  lidless eyes
Slips through the boughs
  and needs no light.

Secret are they and filled
  with power.
Get to your village as fast
  as you can!
When the sun goes down, strange things
  are abroad,
And Death's in the heart of
  the leopard man.

IT was early in the morning, so early that no one was awake except Alida. Her father and mother were asleep in their great bedroom. In the drawing room, three green parrots were asleep in their hooded cages. Outside, the African house servants and field hands were asleep in their houses shaped like beehives.

Only Alida was awake, shivering in the coolness of the air before sunrise. Only Alida was awake and tiptoeing down the wide hallway, her bare feet very silent on the tiled floor.

Only Alida was awake, tiptoeing toward the back door and the path that led down to the river, marking the end of her father's many-acred coffee farm.

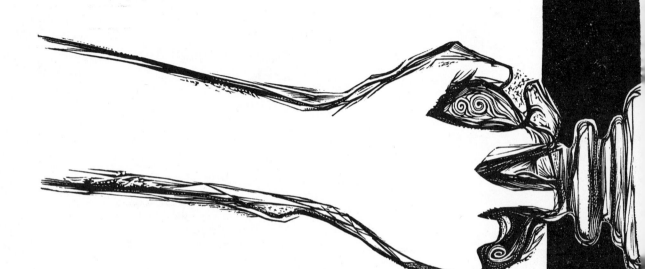

Quietly, quietly Alida pulled back the shining
bolts of the door. Quietly, quietly she turned the
great polished brass knob, and quietly closed the
door behind her.

Outside it was lighter than it had been in the house. Alida could smell damp earth and flowers from the garden as she followed the path down to the water. Today was her mother's birthday, and Alida had decided to surprise her with a bouquet of water lilies, her mother's favorite flower. She would put them in a bowl by her mother's bed, and they would be the first thing she saw when she awakened. In a moment Alida was at the dock, untying her little rowboat. She must hurry to get back before the sun rose,

before the cocks crowed from their
    perches in the mango trees,
before her old black nurse came to
    waken her and found the bed empty,
before the field hands began to stretch
    and yawn!

12

Alida jumped into the boat and pushed it away from the dock.

Next, she reached for the oars.

But there were no oars in the boat.

Someone had taken them to the boathouse where they belonged, but where no one before had ever remembered to put them.

"Oh, well," thought Alida, "I'll just pick a few lilies while I'm here, and then pull my way back to the dock by the lily stems."

And she began to pick the water lilies, which, with the darkness, were closed again into tight buds. The best ones seemed to grow well out from shore, and Alida pulled her way to them. Suddenly, she felt the boat caught in an unexpected current.

14

When she tried to stop its progress down-stream, the water lily stems broke under her fingers.

Now, too late, she called and shouted, but she was far out in the stream and everyone was asleep:

> her father and mother in their big shad-owy room,
>
> her wise old nurse, and the other house servants,
>
> and the field hands in their beehive huts.

Faster and faster now, the little boat was moving.

To her cries, only birds answered with harsh shrieks or sleepy cheepings.

She thought of swimming ashore, but something that looked like a log moved just a little and something that looked like a knothole in the log opened and shut; and Alida knew that a crocodile was on watch for its breakfast.

Now the boat swung altogether free of the matted lily bed. Just then the sun, barbaric as a Zulu warrior, sprang above the shoulder of the mountain behind the farm, and Alida's voyage had begun.

In a boat with its stern heaped with flowers,
> without oars,
> without charts,
> without food of any kind,
> Alida's long voyage had begun.

17

"Surely," Alida told herself, "they'll soon find that I'm gone and will guess where I am."

As it rose, the low sun shone so red that her yellow hair was turned to a copper web about her face. In that light her white dress glowed like a rose, and her cheeks looked like carnations, while the water lily buds in the stern opened slowly, one by one, in the warmth.

All about her the trance of night was breaking. Near the bank, lily trotters, followed by their chicks, ran about on their thin red legs, moving from one water lily pad to another. Midges swarmed here and there, the light shining through their midget wings, and quail ran among the coffee bushes.

Alida was filled with joy, without thought,
like a butterfly or a swallow.

As she drifted on, a fish leaped from the water
nearby, and later she saw a little green snake
swimming beside her. It was as green as her
mother's best green glass goblets. When she
called, it turned its head, and its eyes were as
bright as dewdrops.

As the sun rose higher and the air turned hot,
Alida lost her first delight. She was growing very
hungry now and she thought:

> "Father and Mother won't know where
> I am."

> "No one will think to look for the boat."

> "And if they do, how can they follow me?
> This is our only boat."

By now she had been carried far beyond the last familiar landmark. The country was uncultivated and soon she came to the jungle.

The great trees spread their branches over the water, beautiful with vines and orchids and fruits. The little boat moved beneath them, and Alida was glad to have their shade.

All at once she saw a big old baboon sitting in the low crotch of a tree, watching her fixedly. He seemed to be trying to make out what had happened. His long doglike face looked kind and troubled, as if he understood that she needed help.

21

Suddenly he jumped up and, breaking off a branch, ran out along a large limb that overhung the river and reached his branch down toward Alida. But it was far too short. Alida stood up in the boat, but, even so, she could not touch its leafy tips.

Now the baboon broke off branch after branch and offered them to her, but they were all too short. A whole band of lesser baboons joined him, some on the river bank, some in low trees, all reaching out branches to Alida, but none were long enough.

Soon the baboons lost interest in helping her and instead began to throw their branches at Alida.

This was a great deal more fun for them. Even the old baboon joined in the new game.

Skipping along from rock to rock and from tree to tree, following the course of the little boat, went the baboons, throwing everything they could lay their long hands on at Alida, while she fended off the missiles as best she could.

But at last they grew tired of this game, too, and swung off through the jungle; and Alida found that along with the branches and twigs, there were clusters of nuts and fruits of many kinds. She piled them carefully in the stern and covered them with green leaves to keep off the sun.

Now she could sit and eat at her leisure. The hope that the baboons might rescue her was gone, and so was the fear that they might hurt her. Only the fruit and nuts remained, enough for at least a day.

As she ate, she watched the banks by which her boat was gliding silently. She saw an elephant with her baby come to the river to drink. The mother sprayed the little one with water, using her trunk as a hose, while he flapped his great butterfly ears with pleasure.

They paid no attention to Alida drifting by, nor did the zebras so elegantly striped, nor the lone giraffe drinking with his long forelegs spread wide.

The strangest animal Alida saw was a little Guinea deer, only seven inches high with horns half-a-finger in length, like a toy animal come to life.

"Perhaps I shall drift ashore with an eddy," she thought.

But the river grew wider and wider, and her boat never came near the shore. Now the current was very slow, and sand banks ran a long way out into the water. They were covered with sunning crocodiles, and Alida kept very quiet, hoping that they would not notice her. But one swam near and nosed against her boat, going away again without doing any harm.

Among the crocodiles there were many hippopotamuses clumsily playing or half asleep in the water, with only their noses and eyes appearing above the surface. Once, looking down, Alida saw two of them walking on the bottom of the river, and there they had lost their awkwardness and seemed to move as lightly as dancers.

"They can close their nostrils and their ears, too," thought Alida, remembering what her father had once told her.

30

Around a bend of the river she came to marshes where the ungainly flamingoes nested on their conical mud pedestals. At her coming, they sprang up into the air with a clamor of wings and at once became beautiful. The flock made a great rosy parasol through which the sun shone, casting a flowery reflection on the water, and then they were gone.

It was from behind a tree a little beyond the flamingoes that someone unseen shot an arrow at Alida.

She heard a whizz and then a hiss as something swift and narrow struck the water near her.

Instantly she threw herself in the bottom of the boat. A few more arrows came over, two of them striking the boat itself, but Alida was safely out of reach.

Soon she had drifted beyond the range of attack, but for a long time she did not dare to sit up and when she did, the shores no longer seemed so friendly.

She had new dangers to think of. The river, which had loitered through jungle and marsh, was picking up speed, and the shores seemed to be hurrying past her. Presently, some distance ahead, she could hear the sound of rapids, and then she saw their spray, where the river narrowed through a gateway of rock.

Just as her boat was seized by the rush of the first white water, Alida caught sight of a man standing on a rock, casting a net into the river. She tried to shout to him in the language of the farmhands, but he could not hear her above the noise of the water and only stared for a moment and then went back to his fishing.

In a moment more, she was carried away:

    down

    down

    down

along with broken branches, and a turning log and the body of a drowned gazelle. The little boat rocked and bucketed, and Alida was thrown about, while the spray slashed across her face. She could only shut her eyes and hold on:

    deaf

    and blind,

    feeling the planking jarred against

    submerged rocks,

    reeling with the speed,

until she and her boat, the dead gazelle and the twigs and the rolling log (now with all its bark torn away) were spat out by the rapids and found themselves in a slow and broadening river winding across the plains. Here there were no trees except now and then a solitary baobab, sheltering birds in its branches and small animals in the caves among its pink smooth roots.

Herds of all kinds were feeding on the new grass. Alida had never seen the plains before, but from their descriptions, she recognized hartebeests and gnus, the great-eyed, great-thighed ostriches acting as sentinels for the zebras, and the ponderous buffaloes, with the sinking sun shining on their horns.

It was late afternoon and Alida was very tired.

How far she had come since the sun's rising! She looked over her shoulder and there in the blue distance she could see a solitary mountain with snow on its crest. It was the mountain close to her home, and she had known it all her life, but from so close at hand, she had seen only its base rising above the roof of her father's house.

Now, for the first time, she was far enough away to see its whole beautiful shape. It seemed like a friend and yet like a stranger, too.

"Oh, please, Mountain, help me to get home!" Alida begged.

But the mountain gave no sign, as it raised its earthly star of snow to the sky, where the other stars would soon be appearing; and Alida, turning her head away at last, drifted on, farther and farther from its familiar slopes.

Now the sky along the horizon was turning rose and pale green. The shadows were very long.

Alida felt too tired even to reach forward to take another one of the fruits of the baboons' random and malicious giving.

She sat in the boat almost beyond

  hope

  or fear

  or even wish.

And just then she saw the horses! They were of all colors, creams and whites, sorrels, chestnuts, roans and blacks, spotted and speckled horses, like a moving bed of flowers. African herdsmen, riding bareback, were driving them toward the river, blowing on conch-shell trumpets as they rode. They were still some distance downstream when Alida saw them and, weariness forgotten, began to wave and shout.

Almost at once the men noticed her. The conches deepened and quickened their calling, and the herd burst into full gallop. Pell-mell the maddened horses were driven into the water. Now they were swimming in a solid wall from bank to bank. Excitedly, Alida realized that her boat was being carried into their midst.

Suddenly there were swimming horses all about her. Downstream, a beautiful mare, with a hide as yellow as Alida's own hair, was forced against the side of the boat by the press of the other horses. The creature reared a frantic head, milky-blue eyes rolling, unable to escape. Alida's old nurse would have said that such a horse could see ghosts. Now its pale hoofs were splashing through the shallows with the boat still pinned against it by the oncoming current. And now two riders slipped from their panting mounts; dark hands seized the gunwale, and Alida was almost thrown to her knees as the keel ground up the bank.

It was an old man, very tall, very thin, very erect, who lifted her out. Then she was surrounded. Black men, all very tall, all very thin, all very erect seemed to be everywhere. Young boys drove the herd off for its night grazing, but the men stood about, staring in silence at Alida, at her long yellow hair, at her white dress, at the little ring on her hand. They looked at her as though she were something rare and precious, but she could not guess what they were thinking.

She was too tired to try, and at last they built her a bower of branches, sticking the sharp ends into the ground in a circle and tying the leafy tops together like a green basket turned upside down. She crawled gratefully into its darkness and scarcely roused herself to eat the few mouthfuls of roasted meat brought by the old man.

43

44

Alida was the only one to sleep that night, and she slept only fitfully.

As soon as it was dark, fires were lighted and about the fires the drums beat, the conches roared, and the herdsmen danced. Now and again Alida roused from sleep to watch them, tall dark figures, with long legs almost like the ostriches' or giraffes'. They leaped into the fire-lighted air and seemed to hang there, motionless, their small heads flung back. Oh, they were beautiful, but Alida did not like their dancing. She knew without being told that they were dancing because of her rescue — or was it because of her capture?

In the morning Alida woke to a strange world. A white mist filled the air. As she straightened to stand outside her low door, she herself looked like a white ghost in a land of ghosts. She could hear a horse whinny and a conch shell answering another, but she could see nothing beyond the reach of her hand.

When he heard her stirring, the old man brought her spring water in an ostrich shell and dried meat called *butong*, and when she had eaten he motioned to her to sit by the door of the hut on the horsehide he had spread there. For a few moments she seemed alone. When she saw him again, she was startled. He was now dressed in an antelope skin, with the head and horns rearing over his own head and the antelope hoofs clicking whenever he moved. Beside him stood a younger man, his dark face appearing through the wide-open jaws of a leopard, whose skin rippled down his back. His fingers and feet were tipped with steel claws. A third man had an owl headdress and a cloak of owl's feathers. The fourth man was truly terrifying. He was even taller than the others, and heavier, with a face half hidden in the mouth of a boa constrictor, whose long mottled skin trailed on the ground.

Alida felt her heart beating fast
with horror.
She knew who they were well enough:
 The leopard, the owl,
 The antelope, and snake
 See without light:
 They walk in the night.

Her nurse had often sung the words as a sort of nursery rhyme, and Alida knew that where one saw leopard, owl, antelope, and snake men, one saw magicians.

Now the four squatted in a circle near her, and in silence began a game with cowrie shells. Each man had about twenty shells on the earth before him. At first Alida thought that the object of the game was to win more shells, but once, when the antelope man had gathered a fresh pile before him, he gave her a quick glance of such anxiety that she realized he must be losing, and that the winner would be the one who first rid himself of all his shells. With that glance she also became certain that she was to be the prize of the game, she, the precious thing dressed in white, with her sun-colored hair and her blue eyes that could see the dead.

Silently Alida sat on the horsehide, not daring to move, her hands tightly clenched in her lap while the heaps of shells kept changing in size. Now the owl was almost out, now the snake. When this happened the owl gave her a stare very like the fixed stare of a true owl, but the snake man never glanced at her. The game went on and on. Pale sunlight thinned the mist. Once more in the distance the herd of horses might have been seen grazing. But Alida's eyes were fixed on the game and the players.

For now the struggle was between the antelope man and the leopard. The piles of cowries before the other two were growing larger and larger; there were only one or two shells left in front of the old antelope man and Alida was beginning to hope, when suddenly the leopard swept his remaining shells to the owl and sprang to his feet. With an animal snarl, he pulled Alida up beside him. She felt the sharp steel claws with which his fingers were fitted sinking into her arm, but even as she screamed she saw something drop from between his wrist and the leopard skin that covered it tightly.

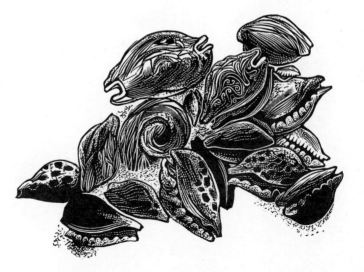

Instantly her captor's foot, clawed like his hand, moved to hide the thing that had dropped.

"A shell!" Alida cried, pointing down at the leopard man's foot.

The old antelope man stood up to face the leopard.

"Lift your foot," he commanded in a low voice.

But the leopard only snarled again, showing his teeth.

Owl-like, poised to swoop, the owl man flitted behind the leopard, standing at his shoulder, ready to take his part. Only the snake man was still seated. Like the great snakes that may wait for days without stirring, he appeared sluggish, but when he did at last move, he moved all at once, seeming to flow to his feet. His great snake face rose half a head above the other three tall men; his shoulders, under the constrictor's skin, were wider than any of theirs.

For a full minute he stood looking at the four figures before him, at the leopard holding Alida in his cruel grasp, at the owl behind him, at the antelope man, standing old and alone, facing them.

Then he made his decision and moved over to stand behind the antelope man's shoulder, as earlier the owl had taken his stand by the leopard.

The steel nails gripped Alida even more tightly. Perhaps the pain blurred her sight, but she seemed to see a narrow forked tongue flickering between the human lips of the snake.

When he spoke it was more in a hiss than in words, and the leopard dared not disobey him. Slowly he loosened his grip on Alida's arm and slowly lifted the clawed foot which covered the thing he wished to hide.

There it lay in the dust, a cowrie shell.

Relief swept through Alida.

The game had not been fairly won: surely she could not be claimed by the leopard man. Would they play again? Her courage was almost gone. But she need not have been afraid.

Already the leopard had turned on his heel and was stalking away, followed by his friend the owl, and last went the snake man who had saved her, but who did not so much as look once in her direction. Only the old antelope man was left, carefully removing his antelope head and skin and folding them away in the painted leather bag he wore over his lean shoulders.

When it was in place, and not till then, he turned to Alida with a smile and she ran to him. It was he who had cared for her, fed her, and sheltered her, gambled against the others for her, and won her. It was he who now bound up her wounded arm. With him at last she was safe.

58

By the time they were ready to go, the remnants of mist had dissolved into sunshine. The herd and the herdsmen, the snake man, the owl man, and the terrible leopard man, once more in human guise, were on their way to their own villages. Farther and farther off Alida could hear the conch shells, answering one another.

Now beside the river there were only Alida and the old man until, presently, two half-grown boys, perhaps his grandsons, appeared, leading four horses. For Alida there was the yellow mare that had swum beside her boat and had brought her to the shore. She rode foremost, yellow head above yellow hide, and behind her in single file came the antelope priest and the boys. Her heart, which had beat so fast in terror, was now beating in joy, and so they set off in the brightness of the morning, following the game trails as they led north and north toward the mountain.

How long would the return take? Alida could not guess. But she knew that the antelope man and his grandsons would guard her and guide her. The long day of her voyage was over, like a dream of the night, and now, at last, she was on her way home to her father's house.

Alida, Alida, gentle Alida,
Through beauty and terror the
*   river ran,*
But safe you returned, the
*   danger forgotten*
With the antelope man.

Alida, Alida, gentle Alida,
The voyage you made, we, also,
*   must make,*
And meet the antelope, and the clawed
*   leopard,*
The owl, and the snake.

Alida, Alida, gentle Alida,
You left for an hour and
*   were gone for a day,*
Or was it a lifetime,
*   gentle Alida?*
Who can say?

The Author

Elizabeth Coatsworth is the author of more than fifty books for young people. Some of her most recent books are *Lighthouse Island, Bess and the Sphinx, Cricket and the Emperor's Son,* and *The Sparrow Bush,* a collection of poetry. Miss Coatsworth received the Newbery Medal for her book *The Cat Who Went to Heaven,* and she was recently runner-up for the Hans Christian Andersen Medal, awarded for a lifetime contribution to children's literature. Miss Coatsworth's home is in Nobleboro, Maine.

The Artist

Stefan Martin is one of the outstanding wood engravers in America today. He has twice been the recipient of the Tiffany Grant in print-making, and his work is included in many private collections. His children's book illustration has been honored by the A.I.G.A. in its Fifty Books of the Year Show. Mr. Martin teaches woodcutting and engraving at the Summit Art Center in Summit, New Jersey. He lives with his wife and four children in Roosevelt, New Jersey.